Little Jacky Yooper

Kid Fisherman

'The First Time'

Jeffrey A. Schlosser

AuthorHouse™
1663 Liberty Drive
Bloomington, IN 47403
www.authorhouse.com
Phone: 833-262-8899

Because of the dynamic nature of the Internet, any web addresses or links contained in this book may have changed since publication and may no longer be valid. The views expressed in this work are solely those of the author and do not necessarily reflect the views of the publisher, and the publisher hereby disclaims any responsibility for them.

This book is printed on acid-free paper.

ISBN: 978-1-4567-5163-0 (sc)

Print information available on the last page.

Published by AuthorHouse

authorHOUSE®

This book is dedicated to the memory of Jack "Little Jake" Phillips.
My first and very best friend on the lake.

My name is Little Jackie Yooper,
And I'm just an average boy.
I like to play with friends,
Share my stuff…even a new toy.

But no matter what I had or did,
Nothing gave me more joy.
Than the first time I fished,
As a very young little boy.

I remember all about,
The first time I went.
It started early one morning,
And all day I spent.

My father took me,
And his very good pal.
He was so nice and funny,
I called him my Uncle Al.

They both showed me a lot,
About fishing that day.
How to bait, how to cast,
It was all just like play.

I fished the whole morning,
But did not get a bite,
But did not mind at all,
And just kept my bobber in sight.

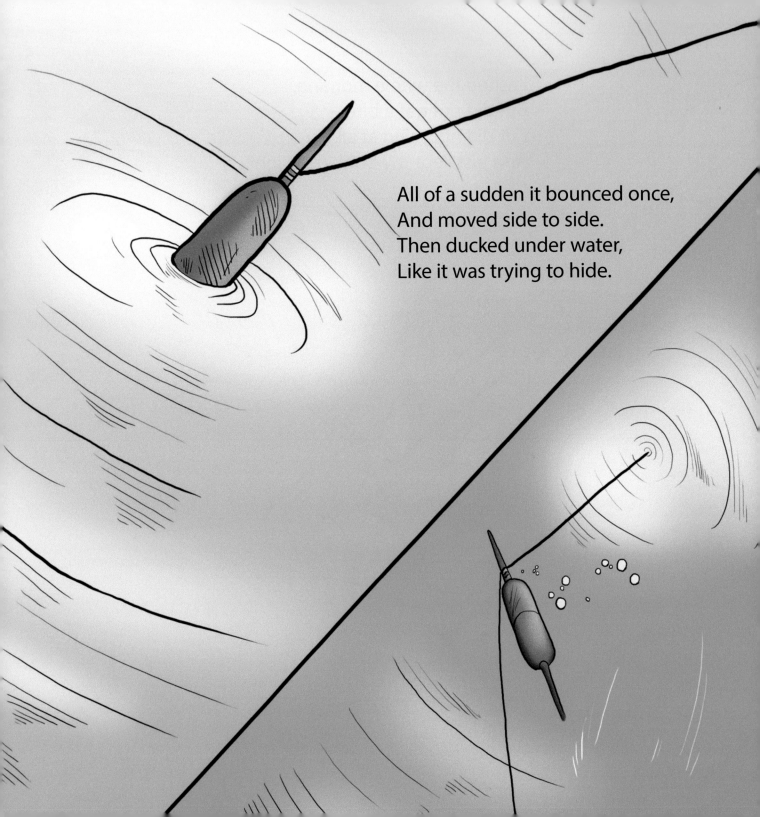

All of a sudden it bounced once,
And moved side to side.
Then ducked under water,
Like it was trying to hide.

I pulled back on the pole,
And the fish started to fight.
The pole in my hands bent,
And the line got real tight.

The fish tugged back real hard,
And tried pulling away from the hook.
Uncle Al laughed out loud,
As the fish splashed and shook.

After a while,
The fish was finally still.
I raised my pole,
And up came a fish named a…
Bluegill.

Uncle Al gently held the fish,
And carefully removed
the hook.

He placed it in my hands,
So I could get a closer look.

I did what they said,
And watched my fish swim away.
And knew they were right,
When I started catching bigger fish
that day.

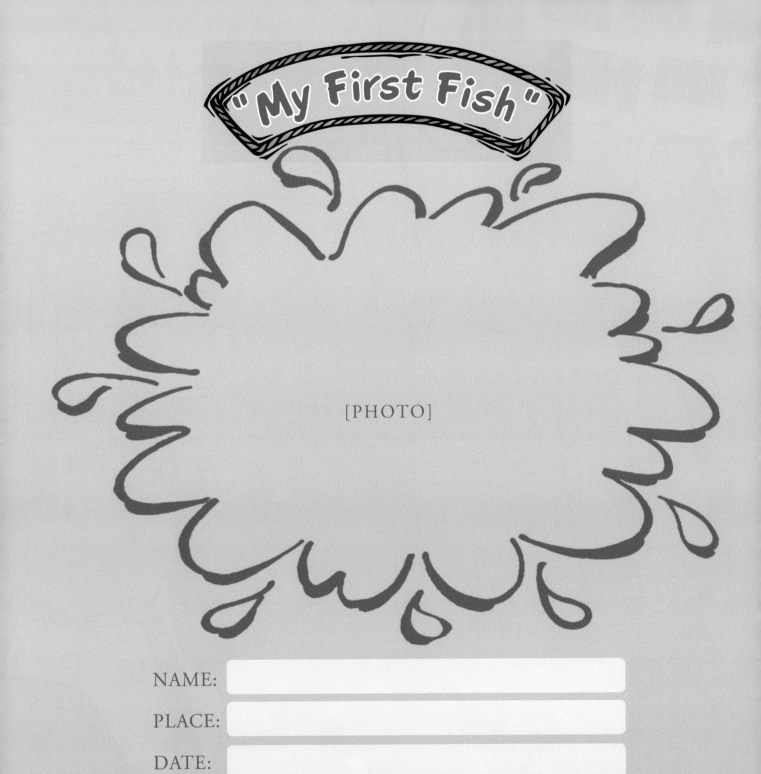

"My First Fish"

[PHOTO]

NAME:

PLACE:

DATE:

Printed in the United States
by Baker & Taylor Publisher Services